THE BIG BOOK OF
WONDER WOMAN™

by Julie Merberg

*Wonder Woman created by
William Moulton Marston*

downtown bookworks

downtown bookworks

Downtown Bookworks Inc.
265 Canal Street
New York, NY 10013
www.downtownbookworks.com

Designed by Georgia Rucker
Typeset in Geometric and CCHeroSandwich

Printed in China
July 2017

ISBN 978-1-941367-44-5

10 9 8 7 6 5 4 3 2 1

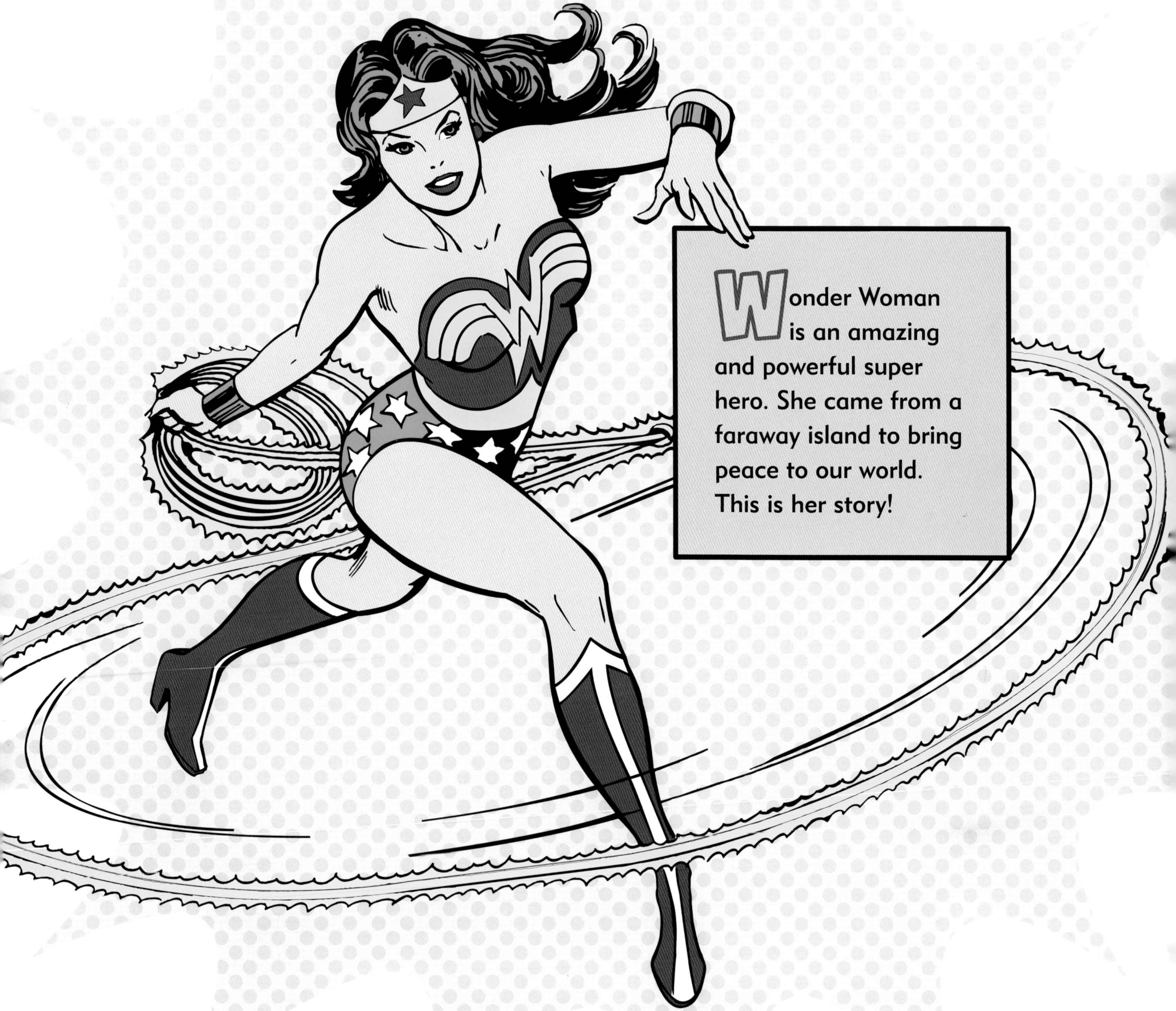

Wonder Woman is an amazing and powerful super hero. She came from a faraway island to bring peace to our world. This is her story!

A PRINCESS IS BORN

Wonder Woman is unique. Even her "birth" is unusual. Wonder Woman's mother, Hippolyta, molded her daughter out of clay! The Greek gods then brought this sculpture of a little girl to life and gave her all sorts of superpowers, such as super-strength and wisdom.

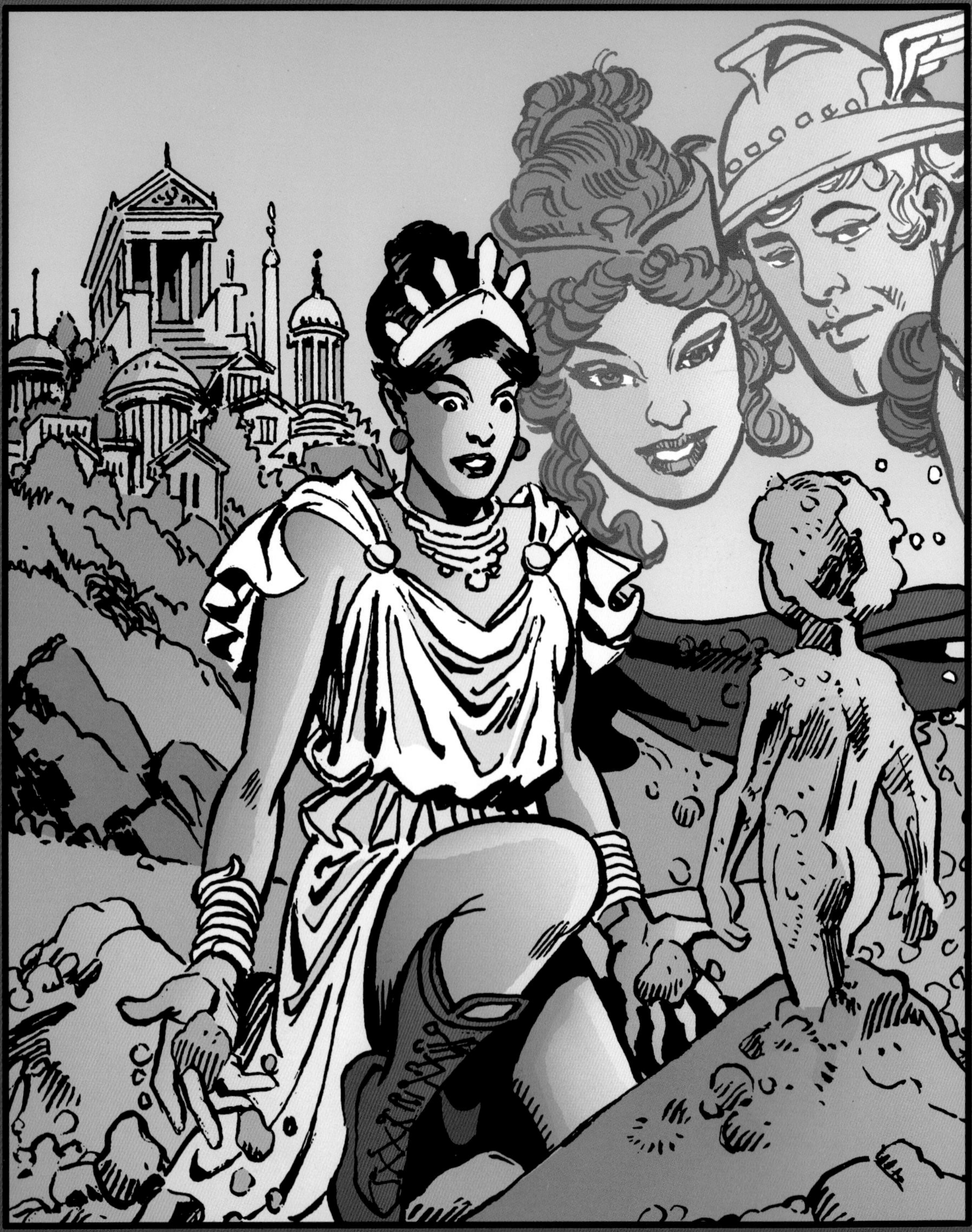

Hippolyta is the queen of Themyscira, a beautiful island. Since her mother was the queen, Wonder Woman was raised as a princess, Princess Diana. Antiope, Hippolyta's sister, helped to train her niece to be fierce and fearless.

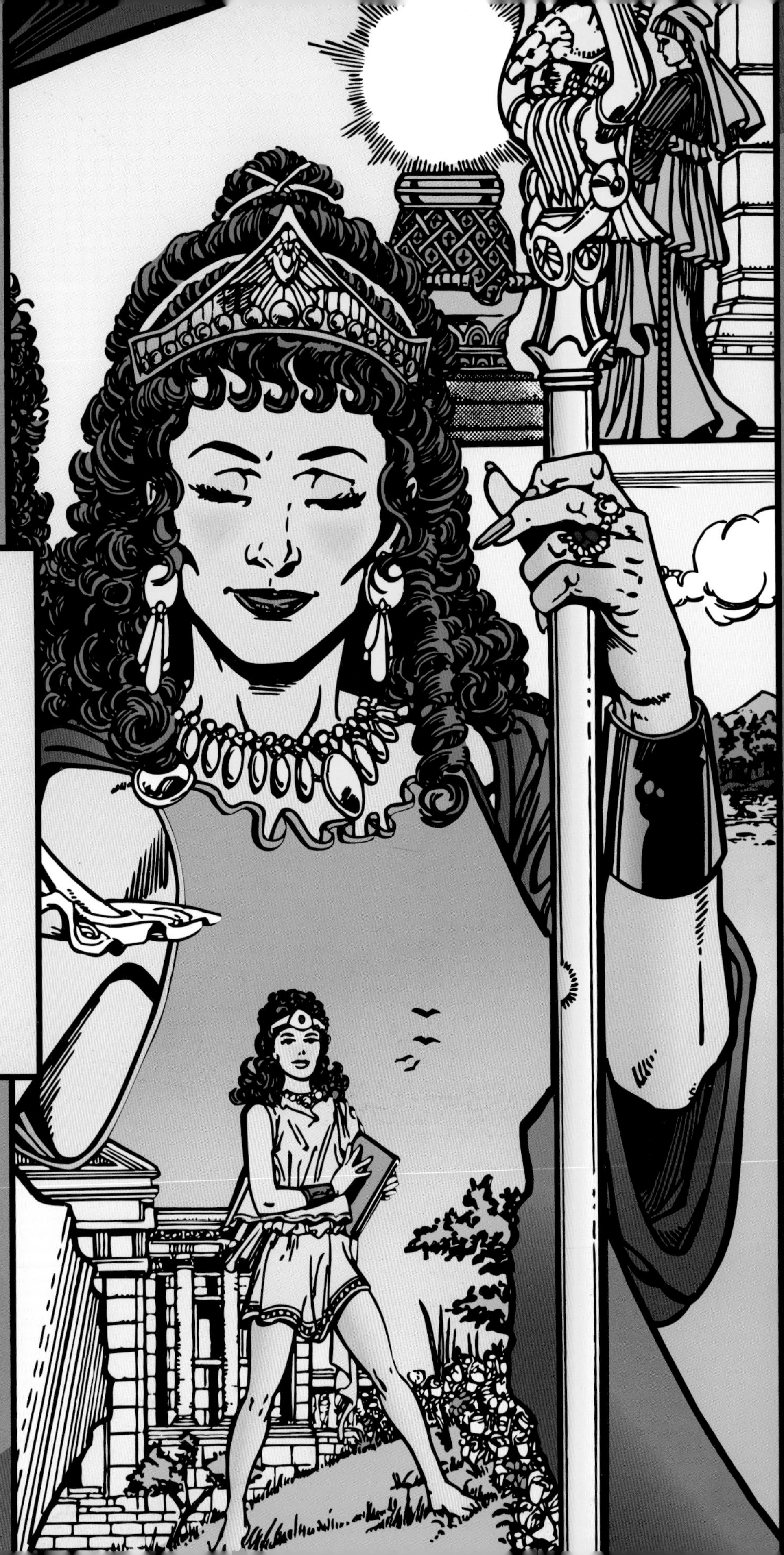

THE AMAZONS

Diana was raised by her mother and her aunt in part because only women lived on Themyscira. There were no dads or brothers—no men at all! The women on this island were no ordinary women. They were Amazons. Amazons were larger and stronger than other women. Diana was the strongest Amazon of all.

Working together, the women built beautiful homes and temples. They trained to be tough, skilled fighters so they could protect their island.

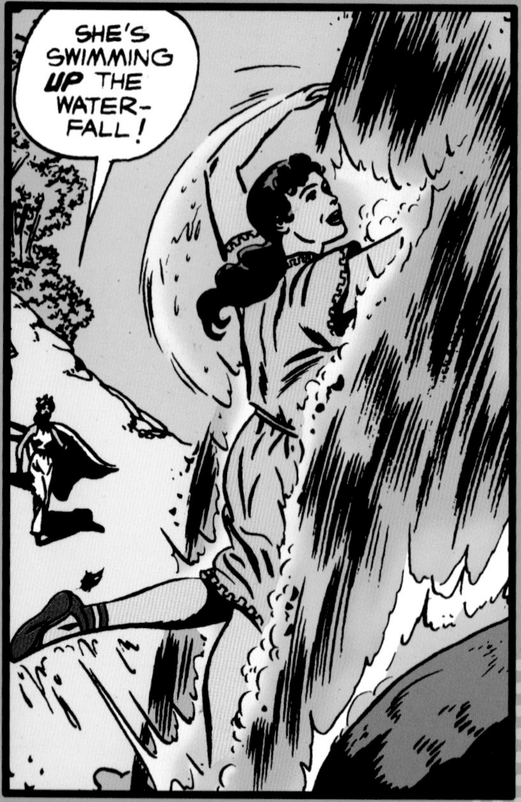
SHE'S SWIMMING *UP* THE WATER-FALL!

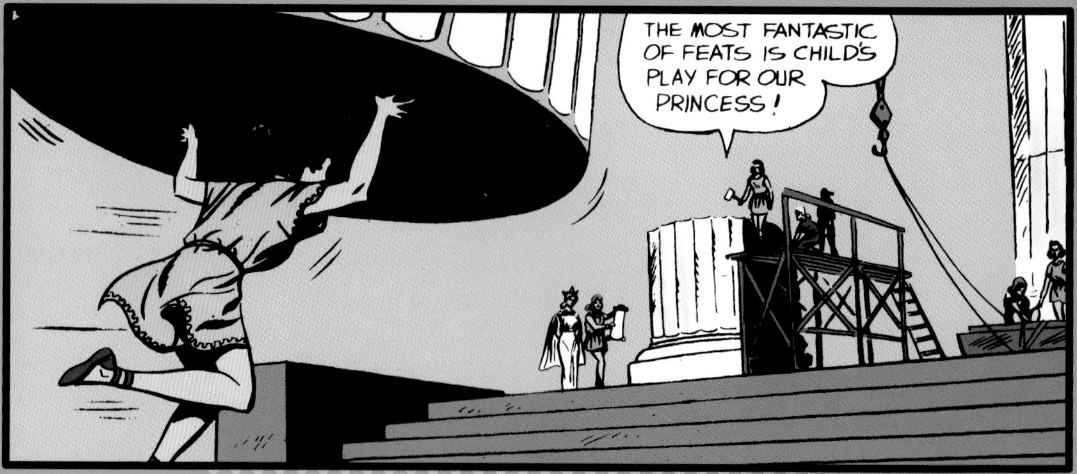
THE MOST FANTASTIC OF FEATS IS CHILD'S PLAY FOR OUR PRINCESS!

Even as a young girl, Diana could swim up a rushing waterfall and carry huge stone columns bigger than a house.

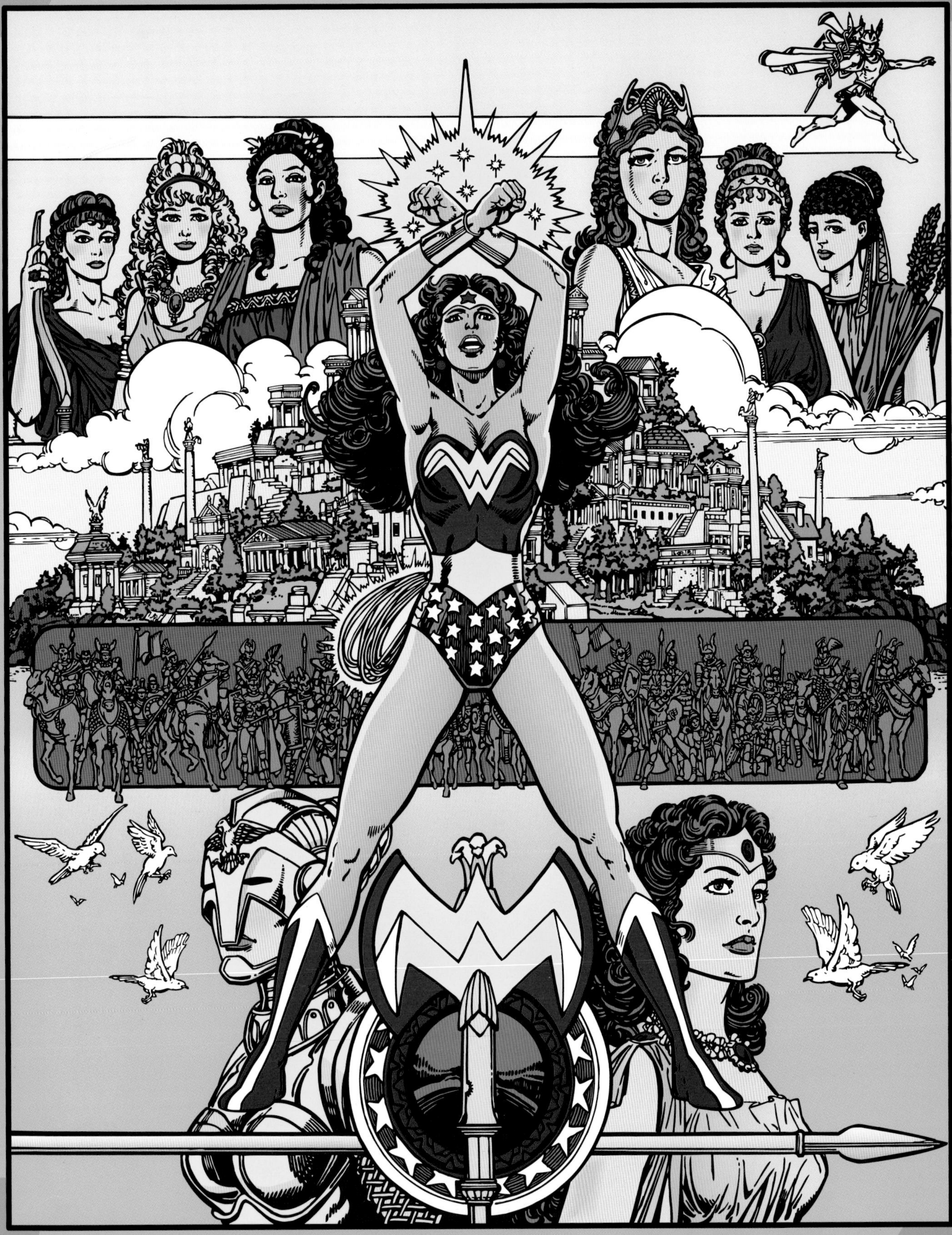

LEAVING PARADISE

Themyscira was a lush, green paradise surrounded by clear, sparkling water. And life there was happy and peaceful. But the Amazons knew that others, who lived in lands far away, were not so lucky.

The Amazons decided that somebody should leave the island. One of them would set a good example for the rest of the world, teaching them how to live in peace.

Diana wanted to go save the world! But her mother did not want her to leave. Hippolyta loved her daughter and worried that she wouldn't be safe away from the island.

The Amazons held a contest to see who was the strongest, fastest, and bravest. Whoever won would leave the island. Diana was not allowed to participate in the contest. But that didn't stop her. She wore a disguise. And then she won!

Diana knew that if she left Themyscira she might not be able to return. But she was willing to take the risk. She felt it was her sacred duty to bring peace to the world. And off she went!

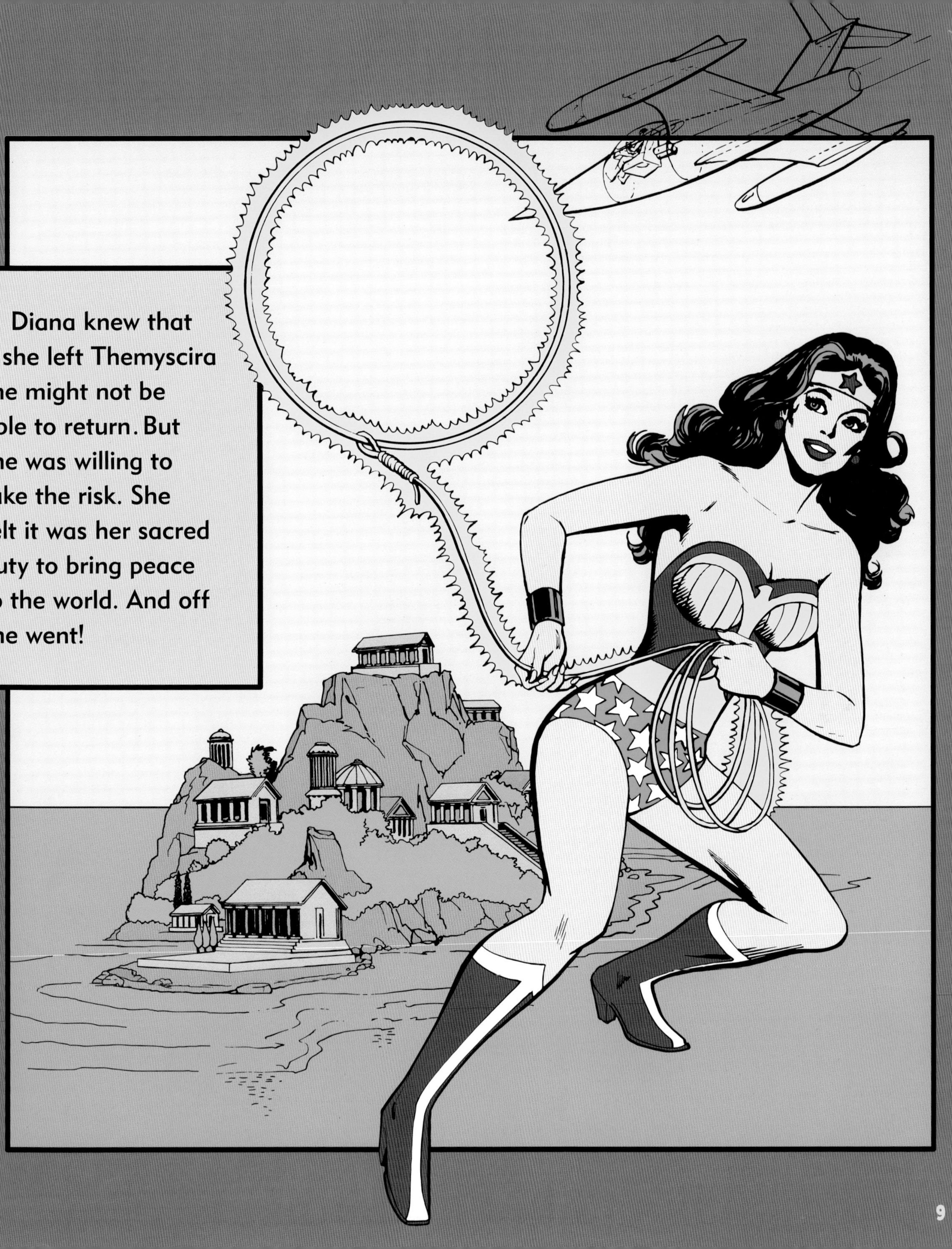

HIGH-TECH JET

The Amazons were brilliant scientists. They developed some very advanced technology on Themyscira, such as a purple healing ray. The healing ray could magically mend serious injuries.

They also designed an Invisible Jet! This plane flies faster than any other airplane on Earth. And no one can see it, so its passengers can travel safely on top-secret missions. And what's more—Wonder Woman controls the plane with her mind!

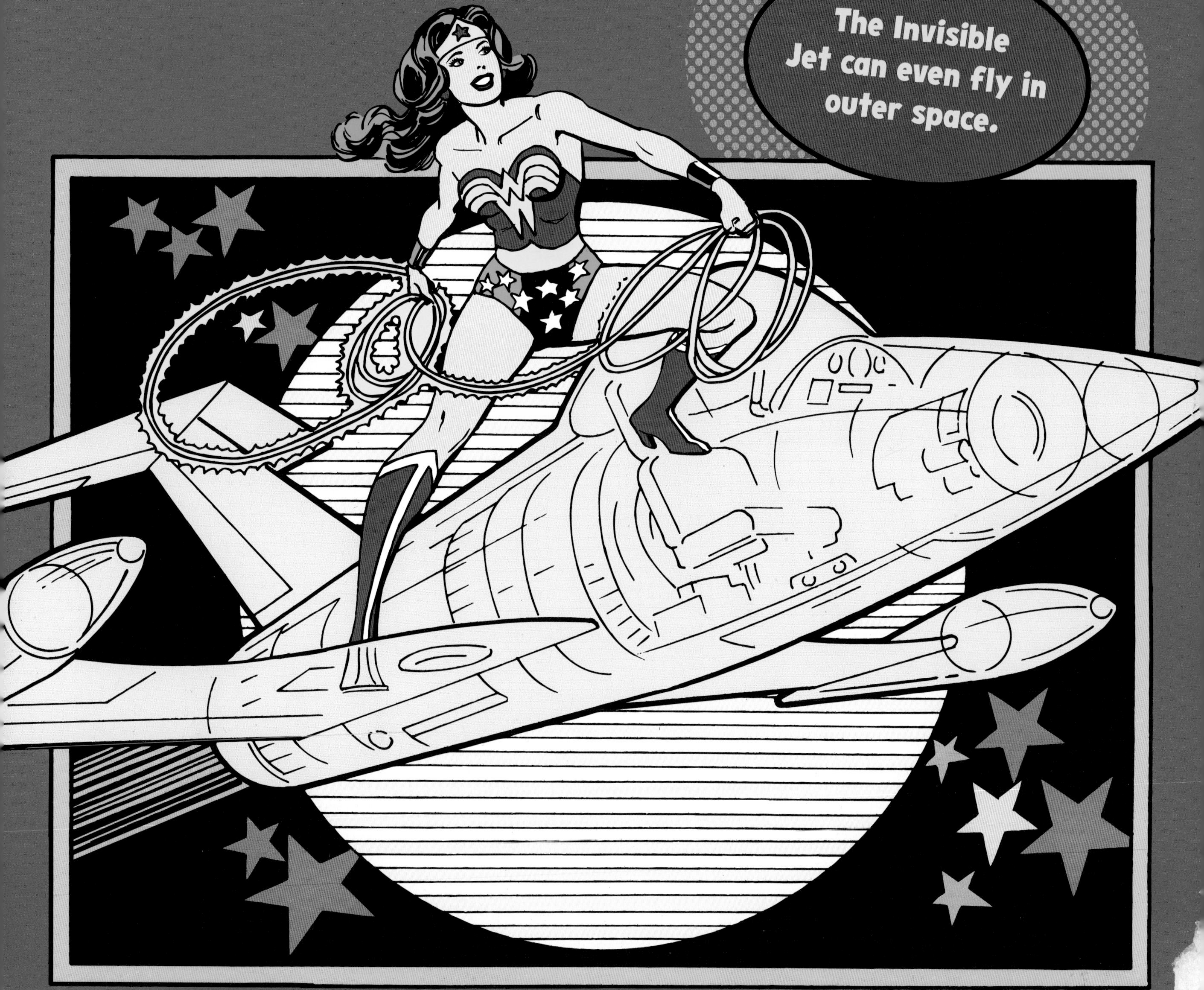

The Invisible Jet can even fly in outer space.

THE LASSO OF TRUTH!

Wonder Woman's most famous tool is her Golden Lasso. Also known as the Lasso of Truth, it has magical powers: If she catches a villain in it, that person must tell the truth.

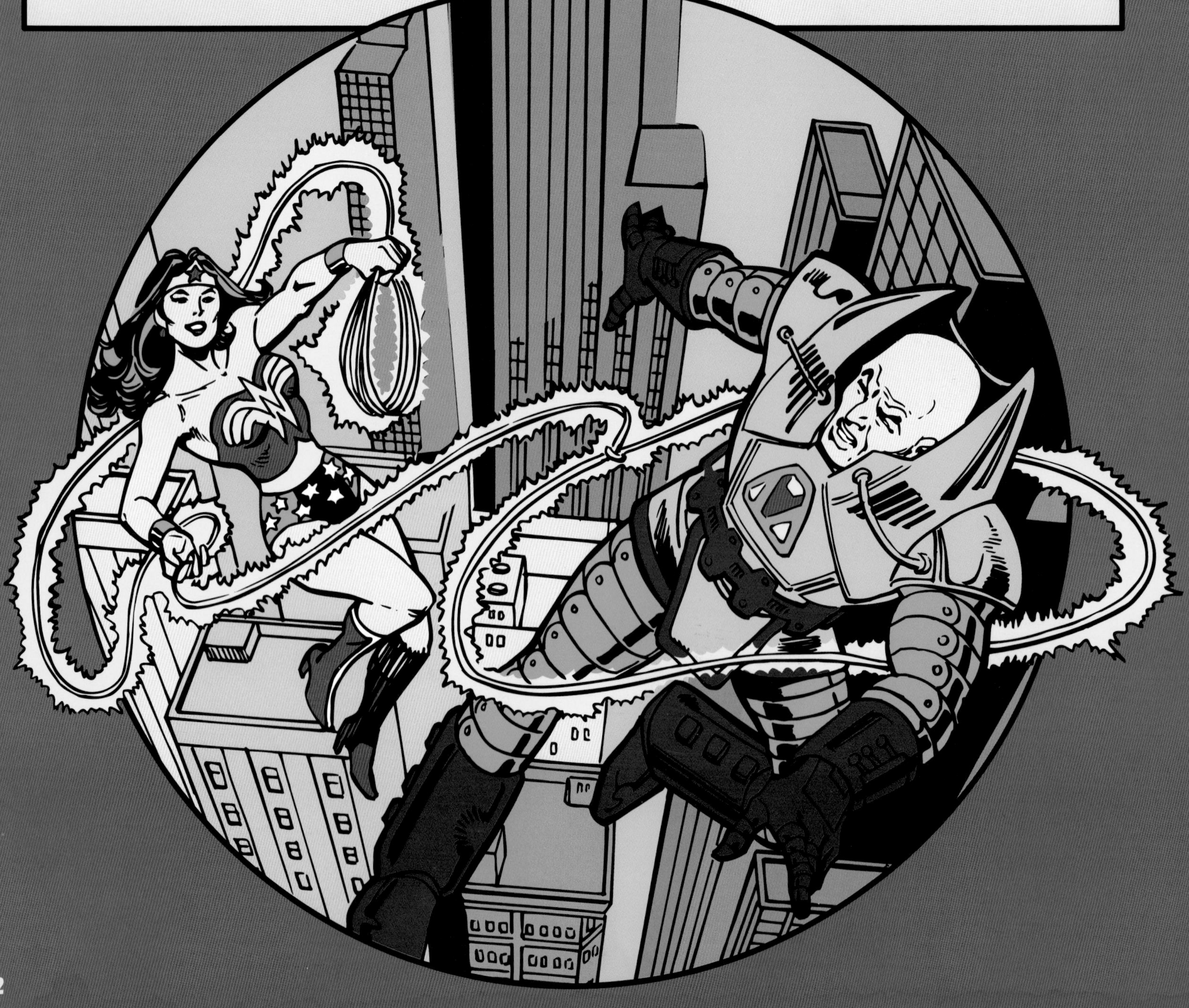

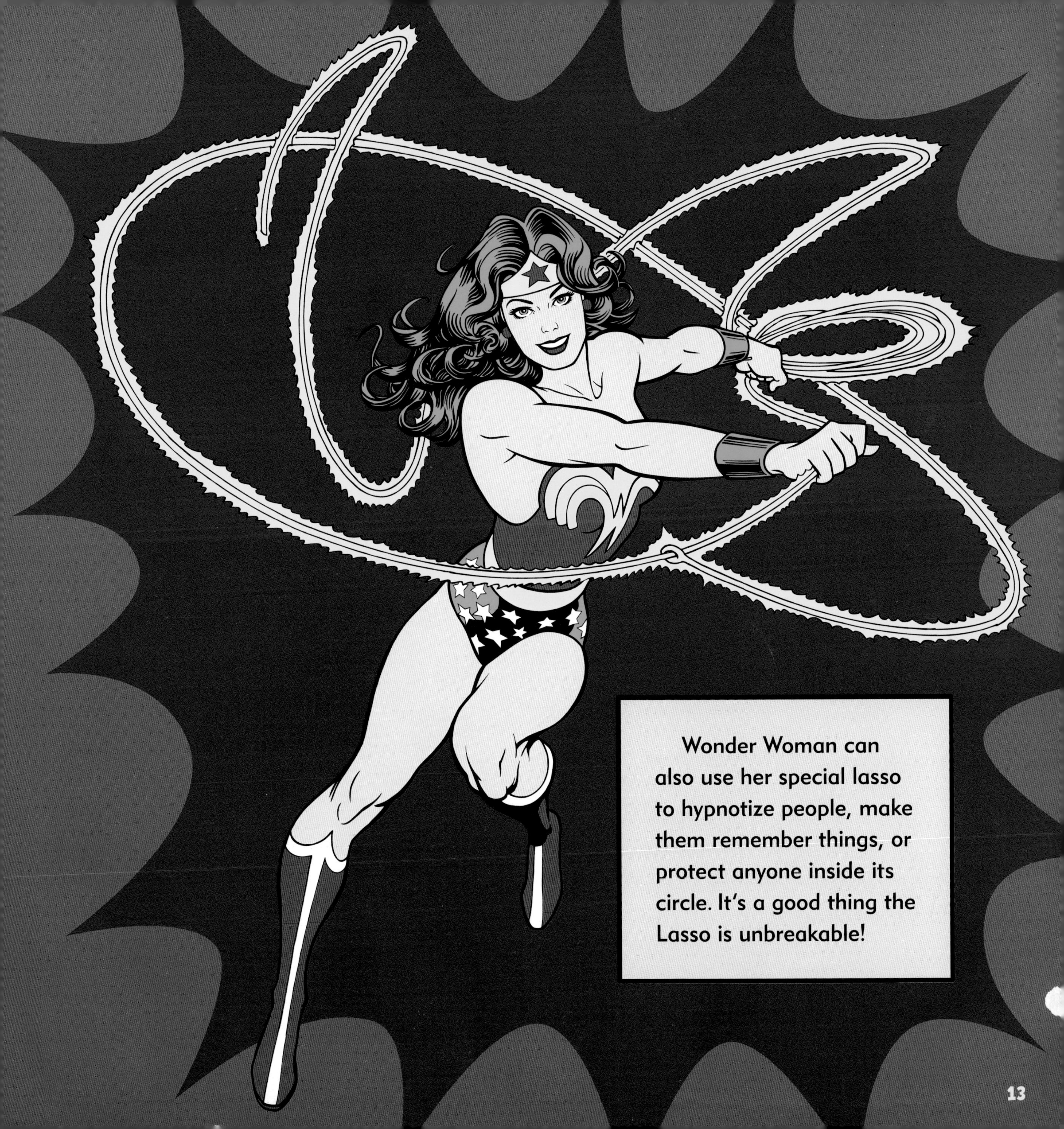

Wonder Woman can also use her special lasso to hypnotize people, make them remember things, or protect anyone inside its circle. It's a good thing the Lasso is unbreakable!

READY FOR BATTLE

Wonder Woman is always prepared to defend herself. She wears bracelets and a tiara, but they are not like ordinary jewelry. She uses her Bracelets of Victory to protect herself from sharp objects or even bullets. The bracelets can also be used to create a shield. No manmade object can destroy these bracelets.

WHA-- SHE'S KNOCKING AWAY ALL OUR BULLETS!

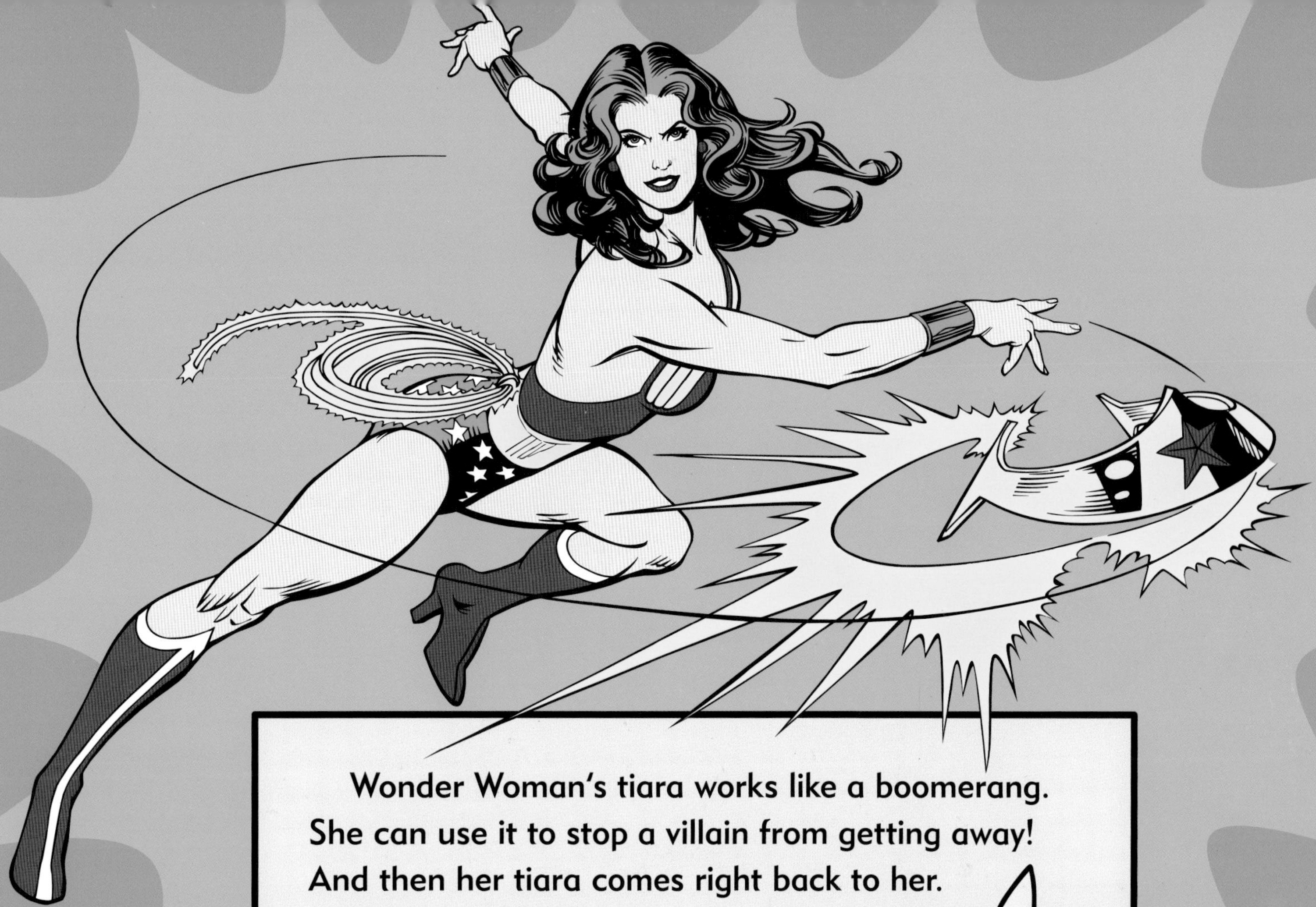

Wonder Woman's tiara works like a boomerang. She can use it to stop a villain from getting away! And then her tiara comes right back to her.

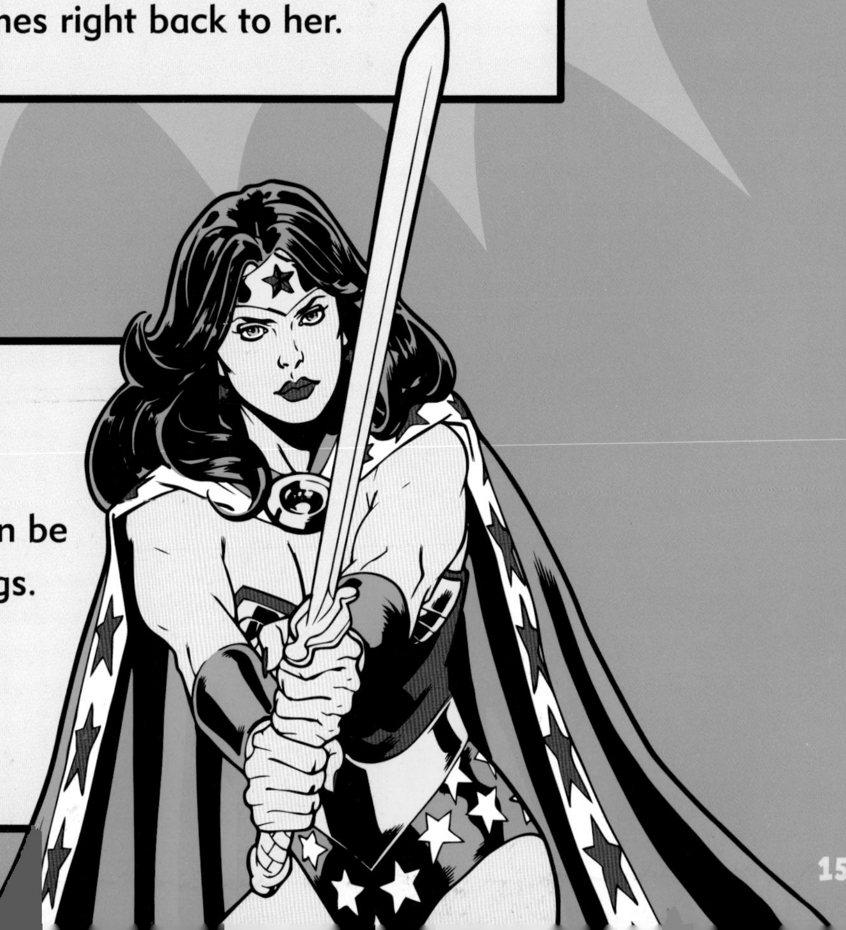

For really tough battles, Wonder Woman also has some cool weapons. She has a magic sword. The sword can be used against other super-human beings. She also has a bow and arrow and a shield. On Themyscira, she trained to use all of these weapons.

MEET DIANA PRINCE

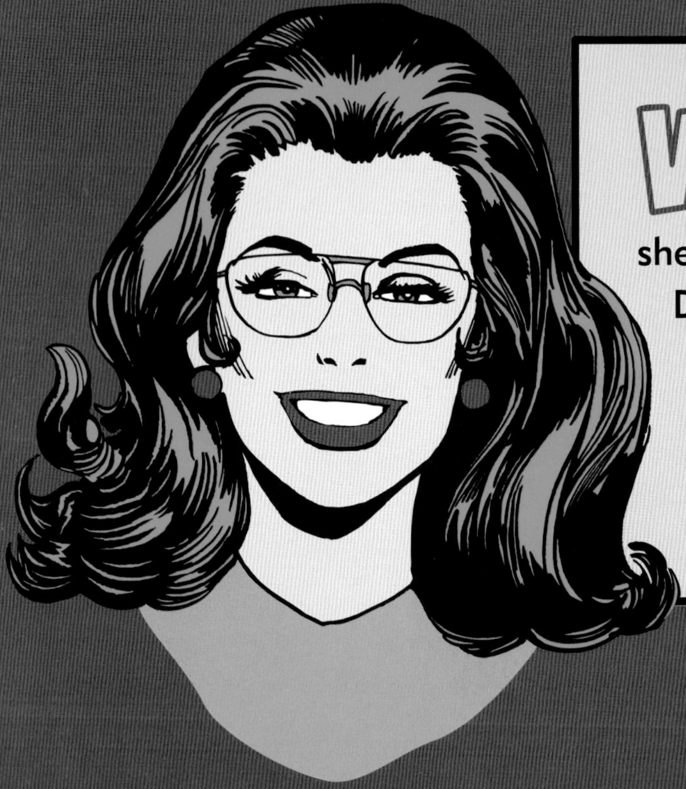

Wonder Woman took the name Diana Prince when she came to America. When she wasn't saving the world as Wonder Woman, Diana Prince worked as an Army nurse and even as a spy. Hidden behind eyeglasses and a military uniform, Diana used her jobs to get information about missions where Wonder Woman could lend a hand.

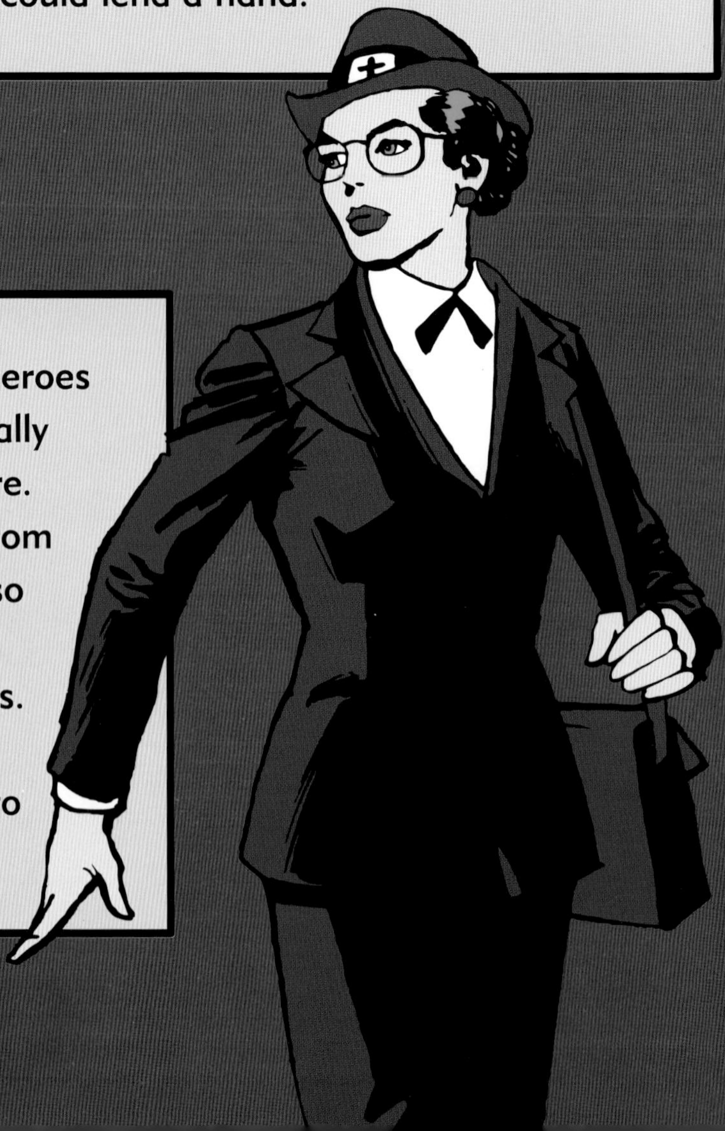

Like Wonder Woman, many other super heroes have secret identities so that people (especially their enemies) don't know who they really are. This helps protect their friends and family from villains who may want to hurt them. (It is also the reason many super heroes wear masks!) Superman and Batman have secret identities. Superman hangs out with regular people as reporter Clark Kent. And Batman is known to Gotham City as billionaire Bruce Wayne.

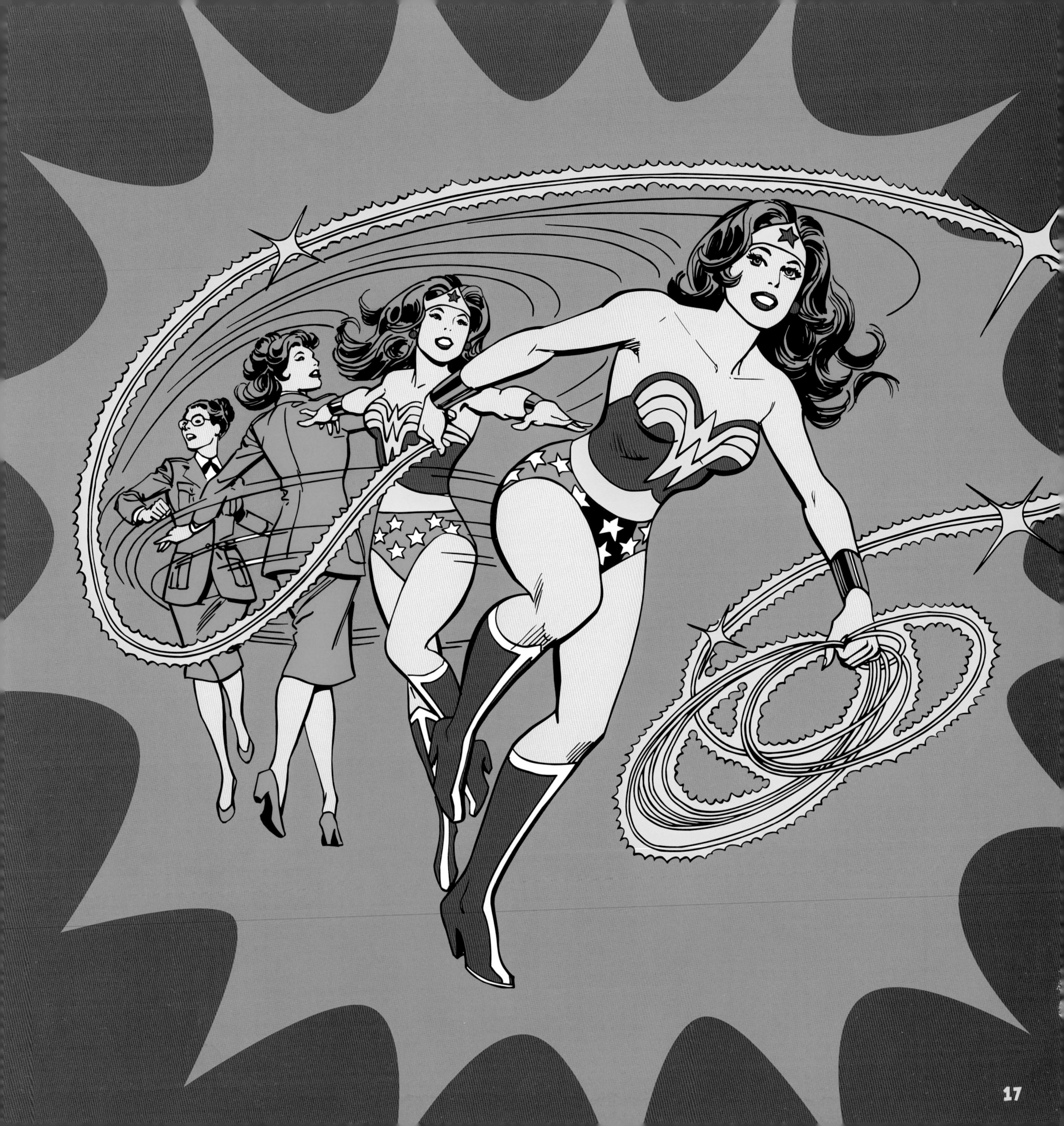

SPECIAL POWERS

Wonder Woman has lots of incredible powers. Her super-strength enables her to lift and throw huge, heavy objects, like cars or boulders. Her super-speed means she can run faster (much faster) than ordinary human beings. She can jump huge distances, and she learned to fly using air currents.

Wonder Woman would much rather keep things peaceful. But when she has to fight, these powers and her amazing combat skills make her unbeatable. If she does ever get hurt, she is able to quickly heal herself—another special power.

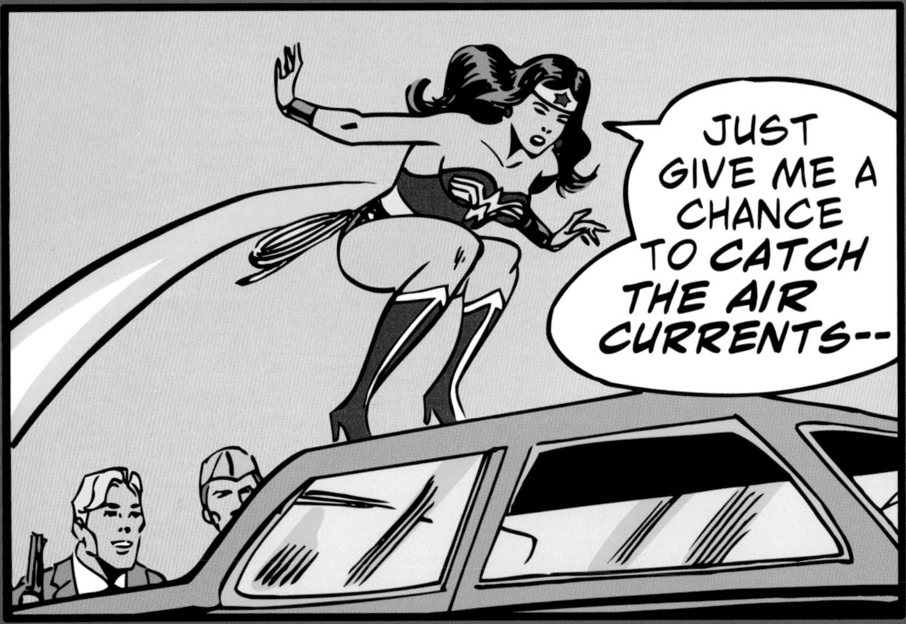
JUST GIVE ME A CHANCE TO CATCH THE AIR CURRENTS--

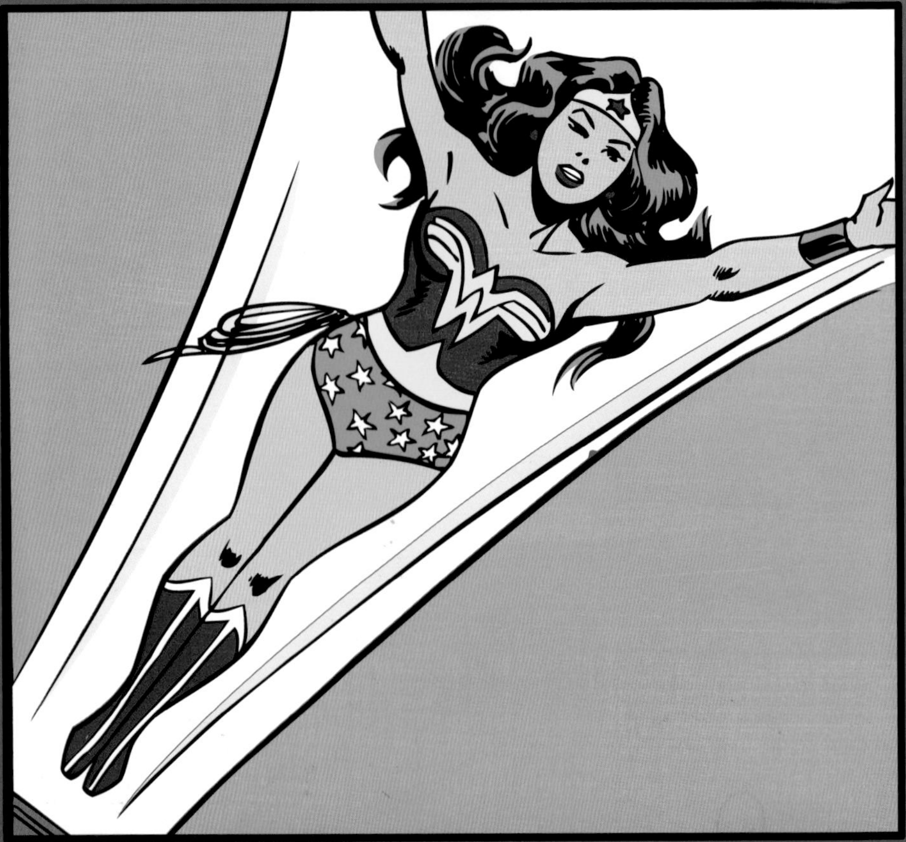

Wonder Woman uses her super-strength and enhanced agility to battle evildoers, protect people, or even to stop a speeding train!

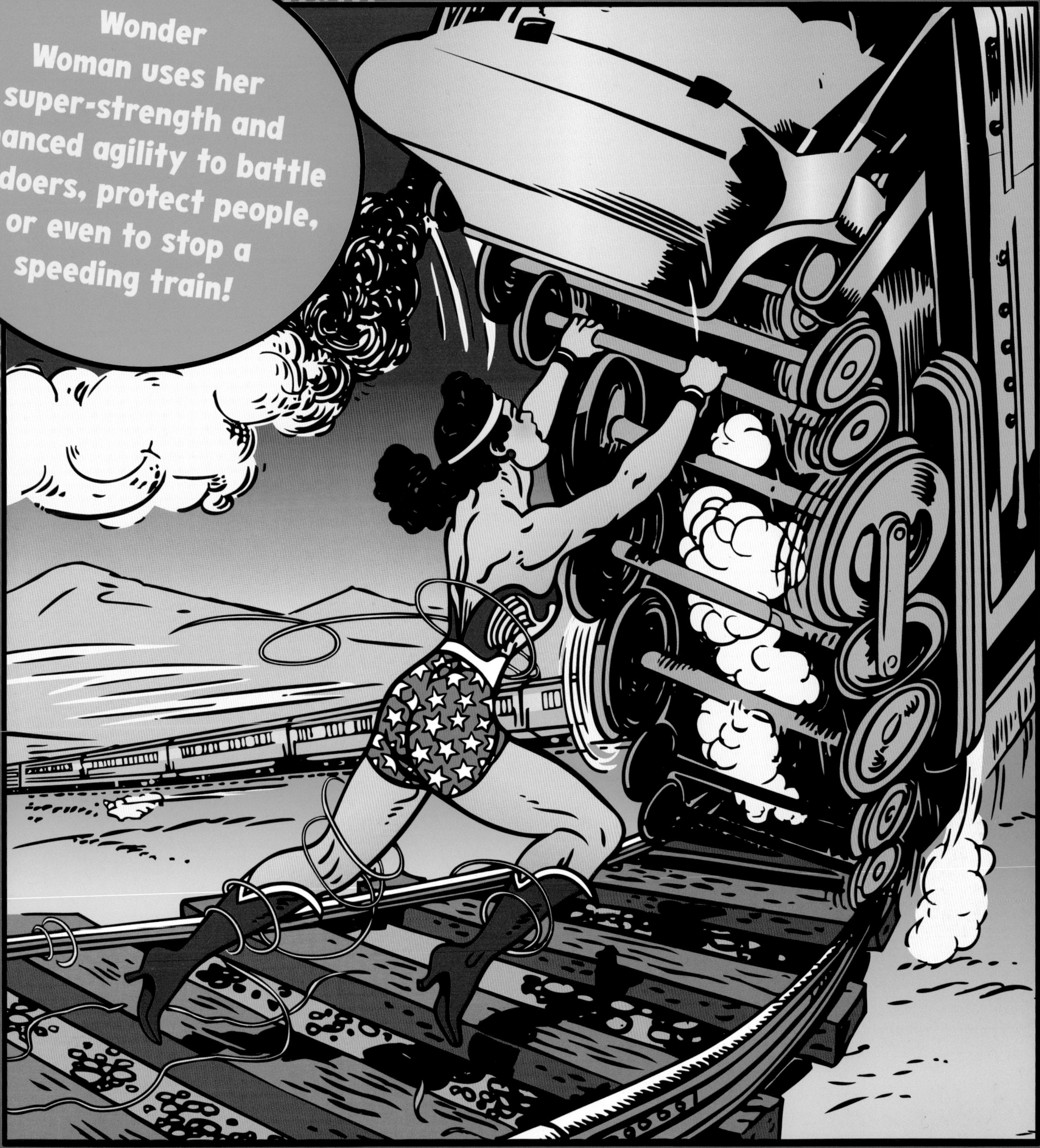

EVEN SUPER HEROES WORK HARD!

While some of Wonder Woman's powers were given to her by the gods, she had to work really hard to build other skills. She trained in martial arts so she would be a strong and strategic fighter. Martial arts, such as karate, require a lot of focus. She had to practice her moves to master her combat skills.

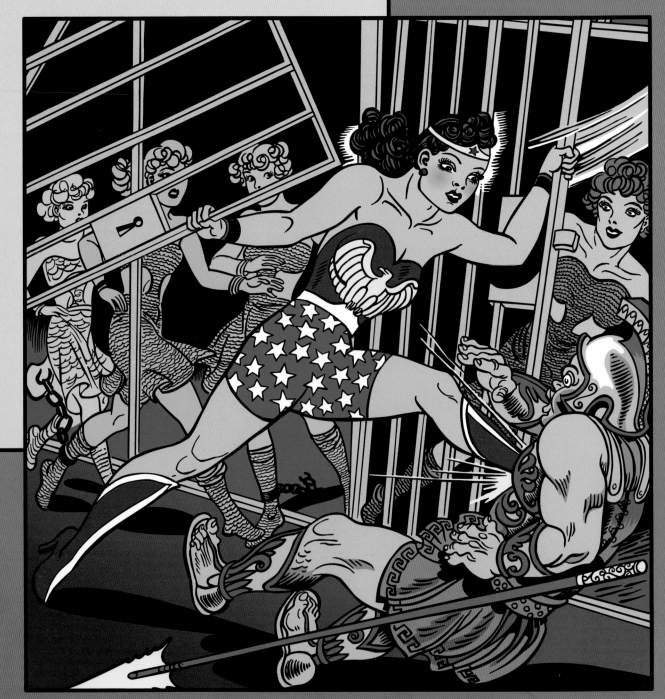

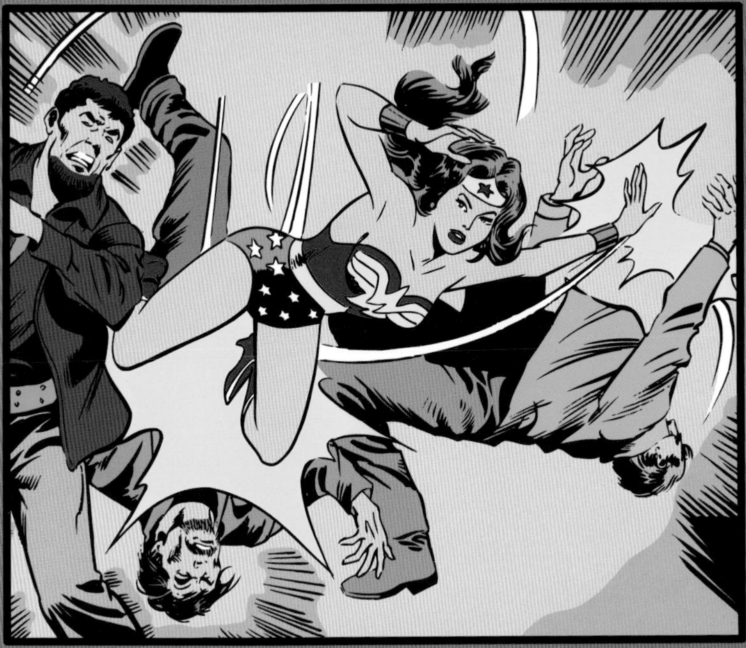

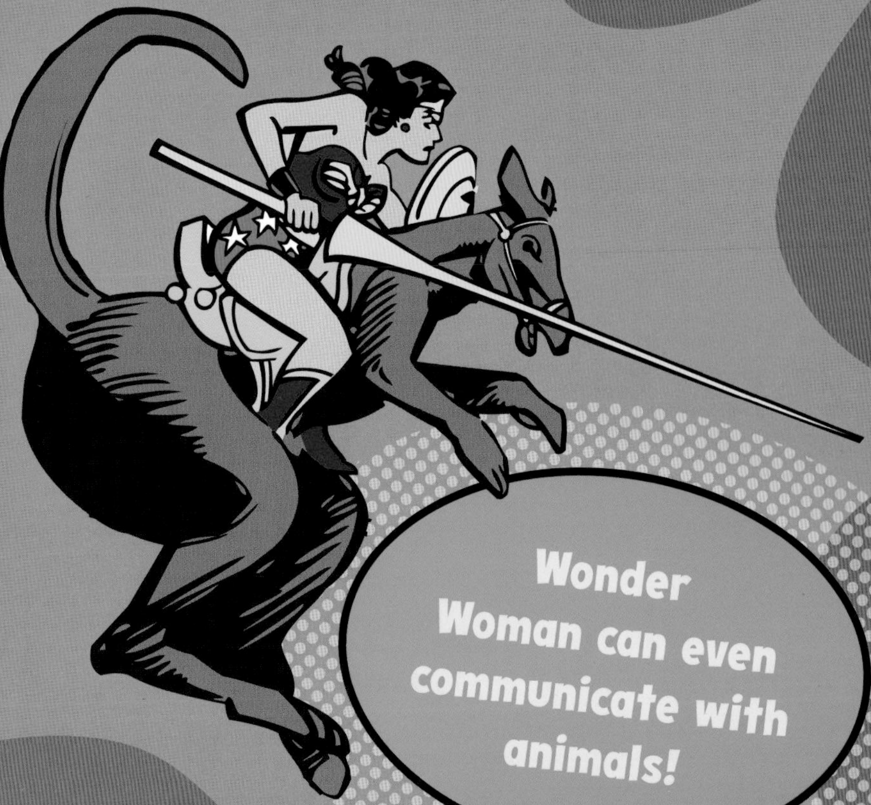

Wonder Woman can even communicate with animals!

Wonder Woman is so powerful that sometimes people forget that she's also really smart. Her wisdom is a superpower! And she works hard to keep her mental powers sharp. One of the things she has learned to do is to communicate with people no matter what language they speak. Learning to speak in different languages takes a lot of brain power. Wonder Woman speaks more than 100 different languages!

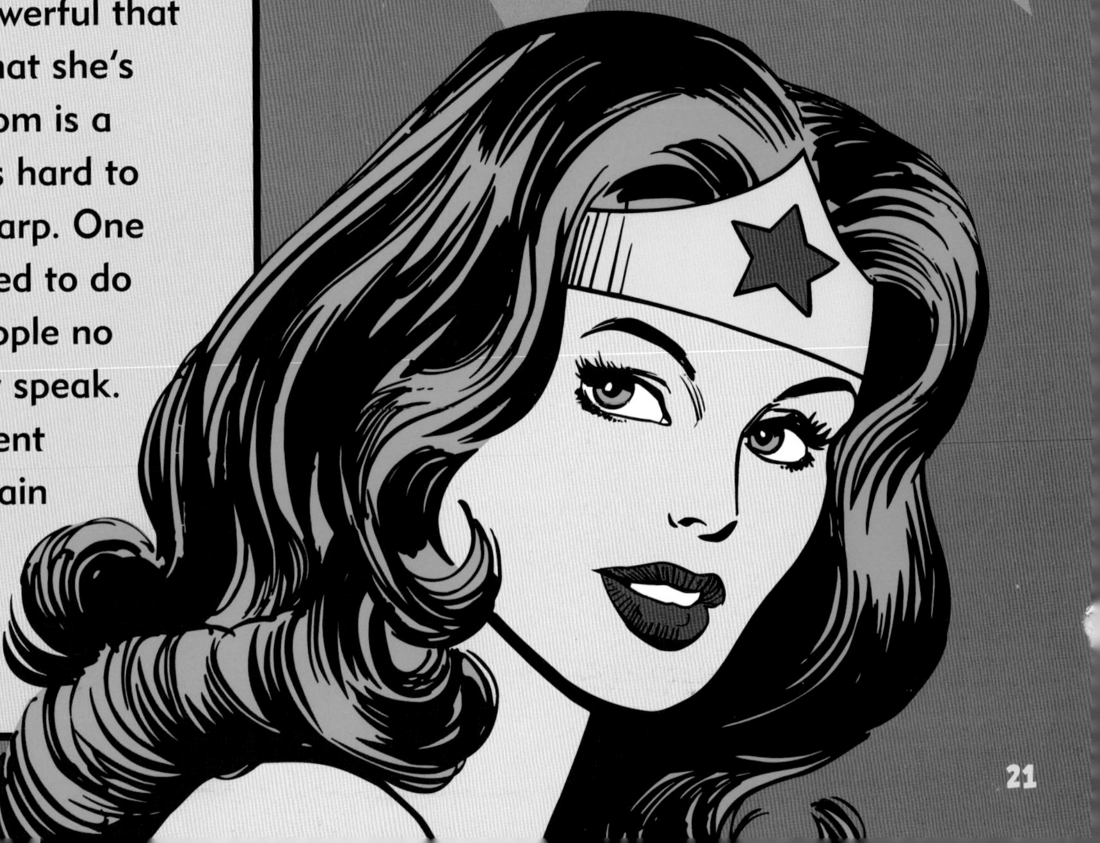

STRONGER TOGETHER

Wonder Woman is independent. She can definitely take care of herself (and others). But she also enjoys working with powerful friends, including Zatanna, Black Canary, Batgirl, and Hawkgirl.

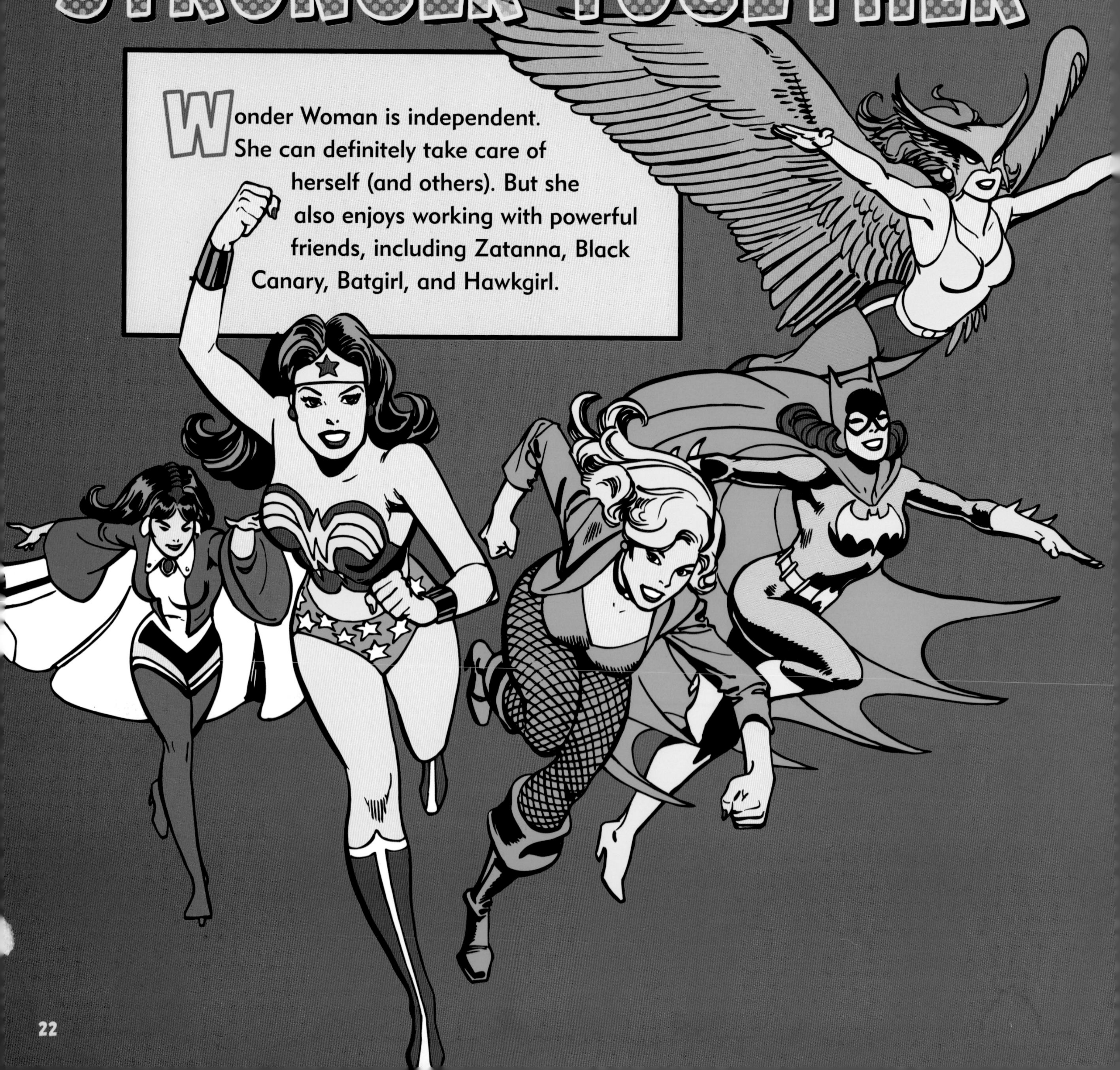

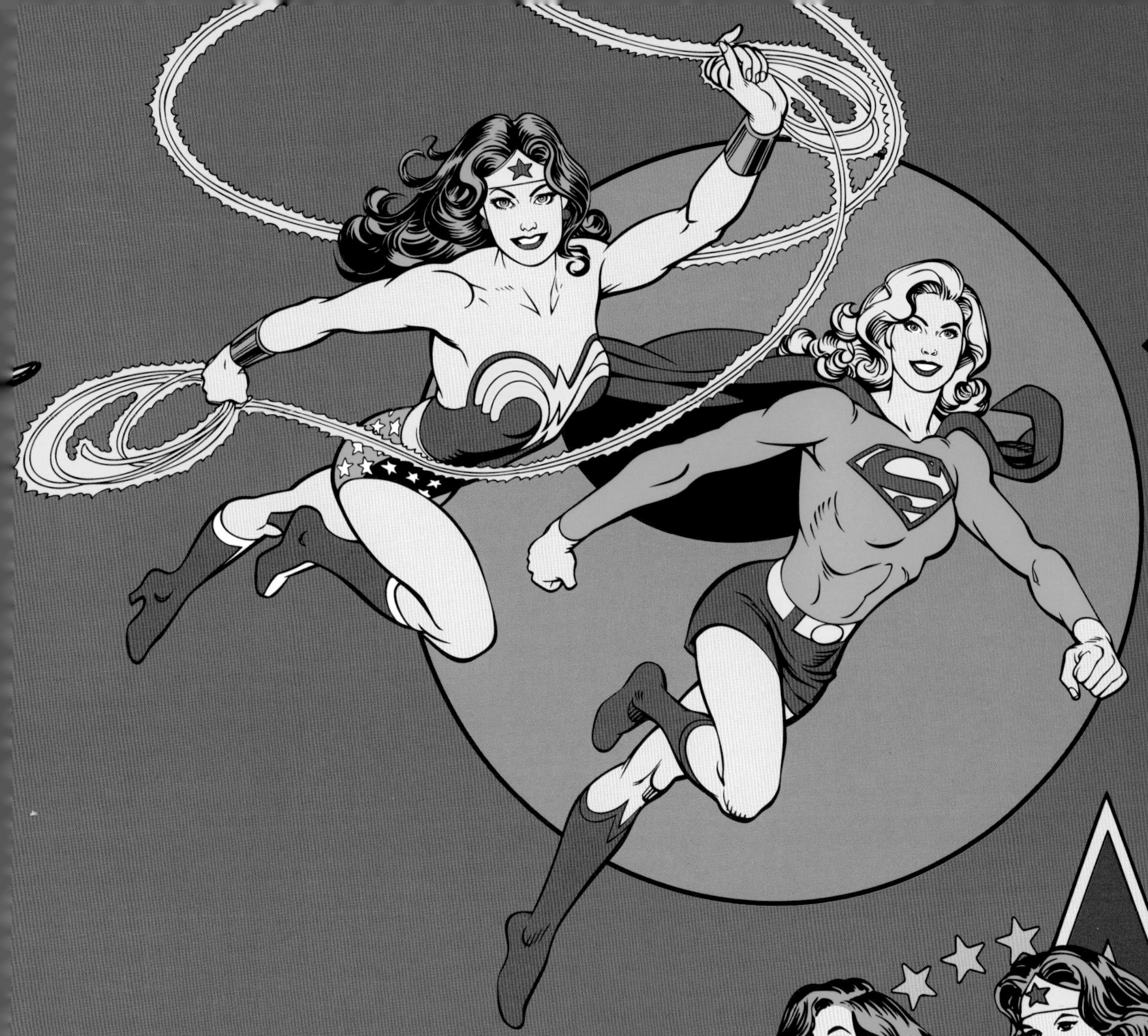

SUPERGIRL

Wonder Woman helped to train Supergirl in combat. When they combine their super-strength and other powers, they are unbeatable.

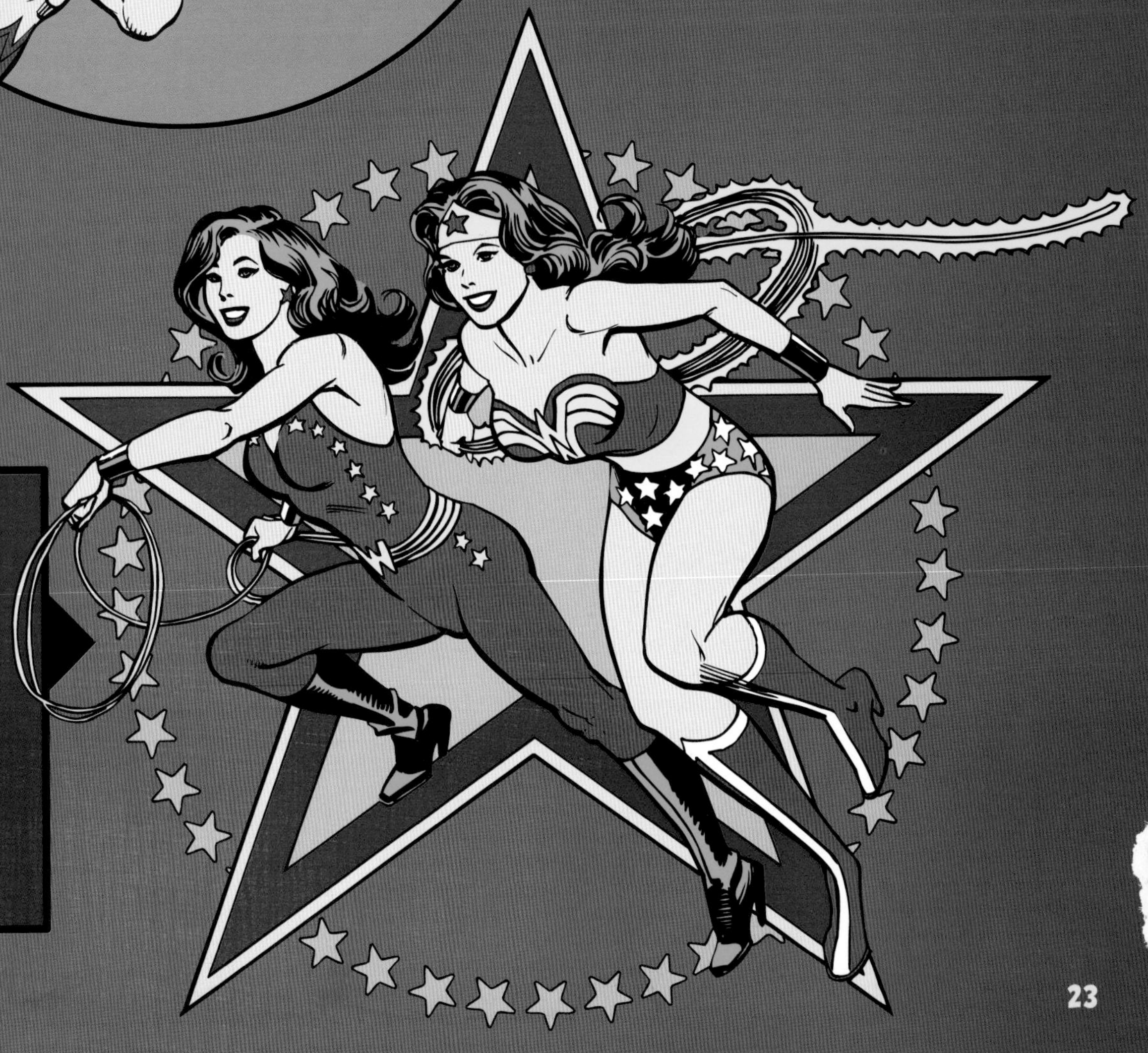

WONDER GIRL

Wonder Woman thinks of Wonder Girl as a little sister. She taught her young friend self-defense.

Wonder Woman also works closely with her super hero friends who have different superpowers and skills. Superman's X-ray vision and heat vision come in handy. Batman is a master of technology. The Flash is the Fastest Man Alive. Green Lantern has a really powerful ring. Martian Manhunter can read minds. And Cyborg, who is part robot, has a brain that works like a computer. Wonder Woman knows that working with other powerful, smart super heroes enables all of them to do more good.

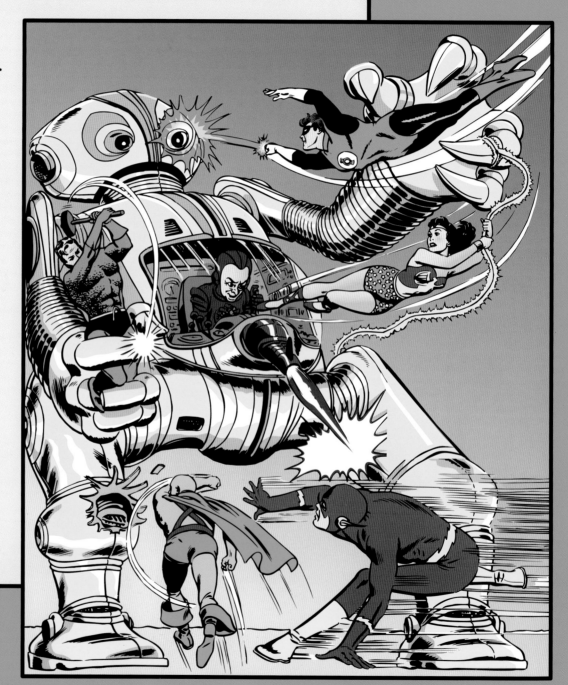

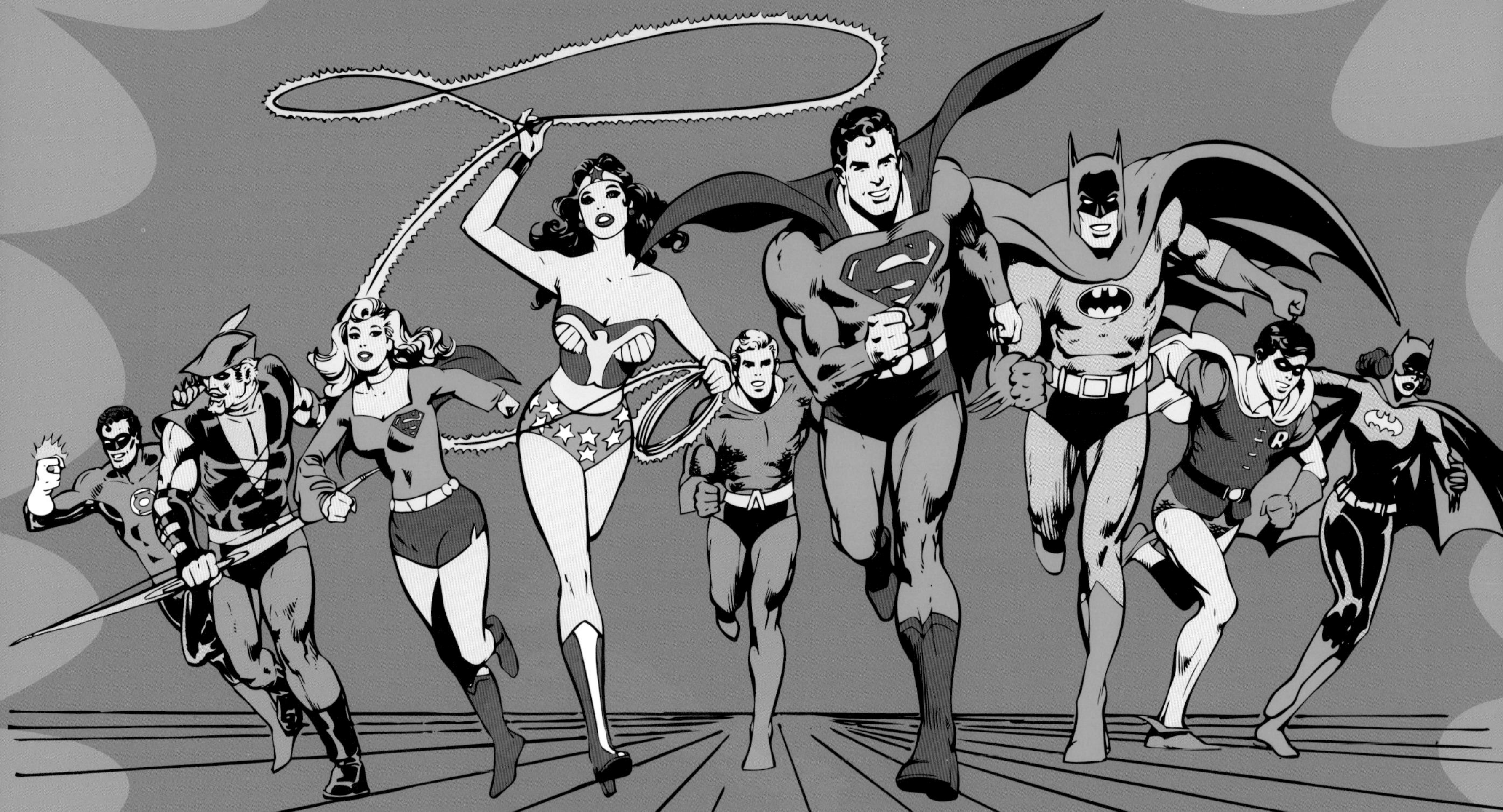

Together with these friends, Wonder Woman helped to form the Justice League—an unstoppable team of super heroes.

THE VILLAINS

It's lucky Wonder Woman has so many good friends. She also has her share of enemies!

She has battled villains from all over the world. She has even taken on a giant alien starfish (Starro)!

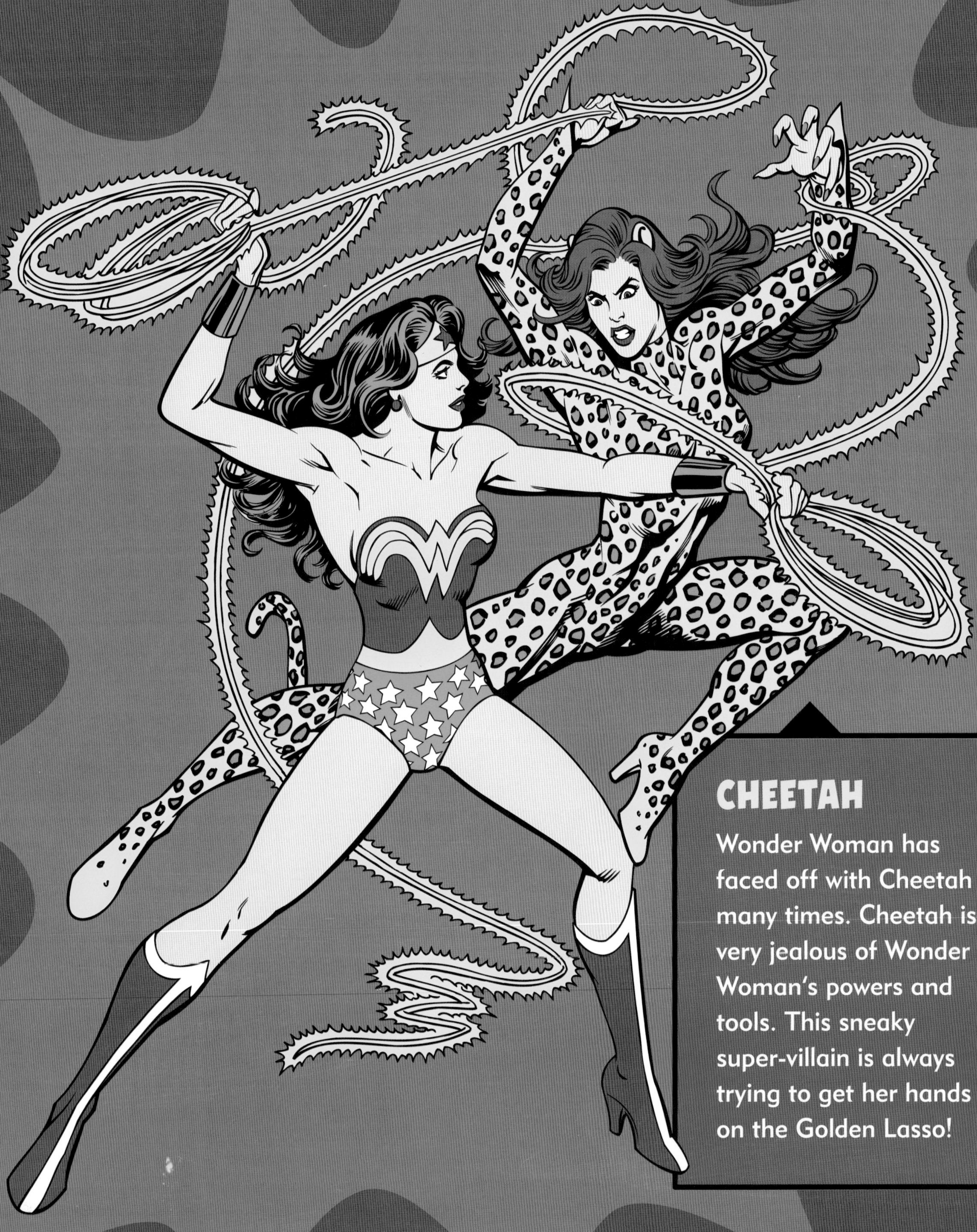

CHEETAH

Wonder Woman has faced off with Cheetah many times. Cheetah is very jealous of Wonder Woman's powers and tools. This sneaky super-villain is always trying to get her hands on the Golden Lasso!

A HELPING HAND

While villains use their powers to do harm, Wonder Woman has always used her gifts to help people.

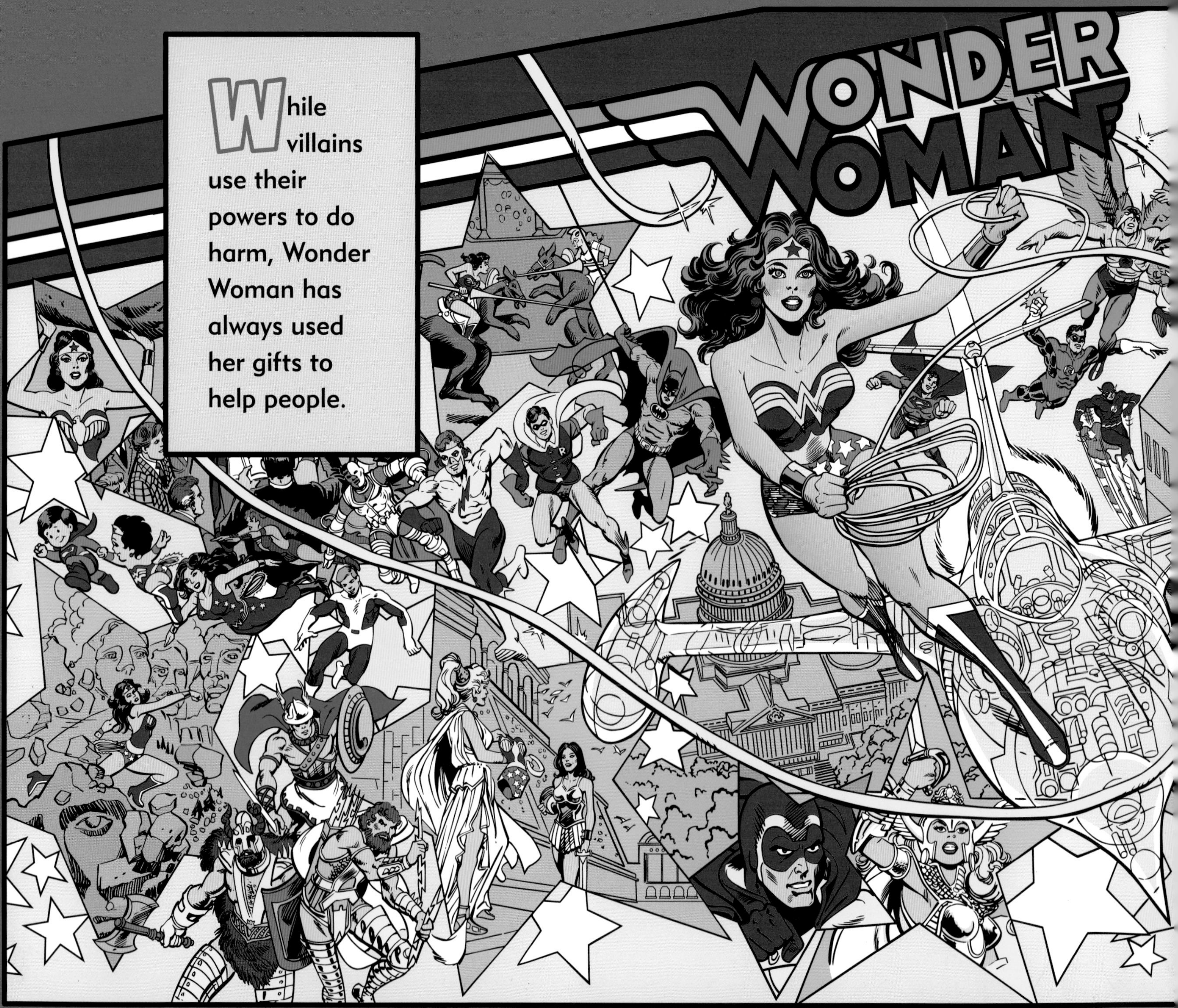
WONDER WOMAN

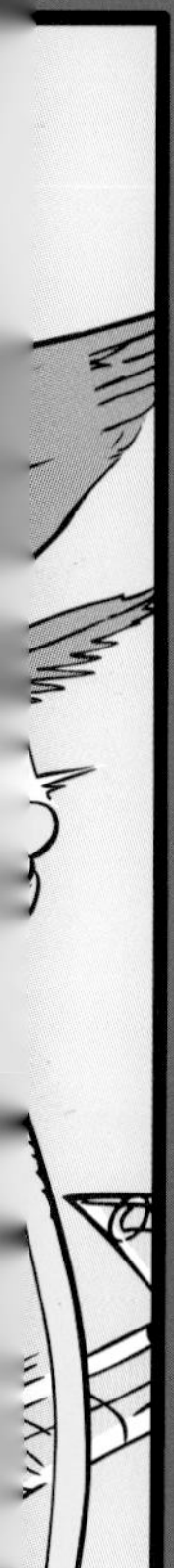

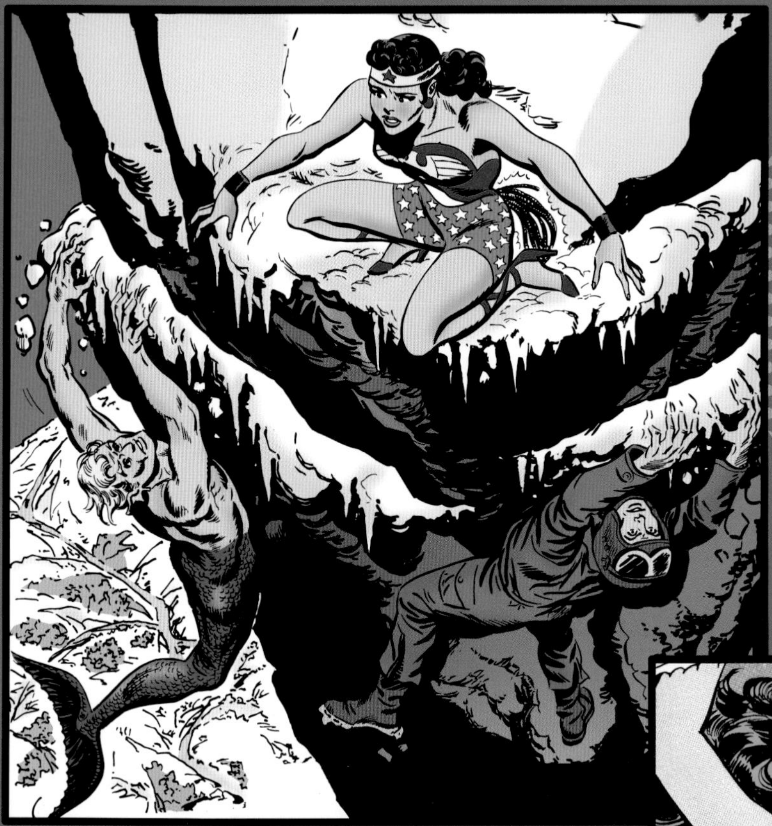

Wonder Woman has saved many men, women, and children—and lent a hand to her super hero friends as well.

Whenever people need help, they know who to call!

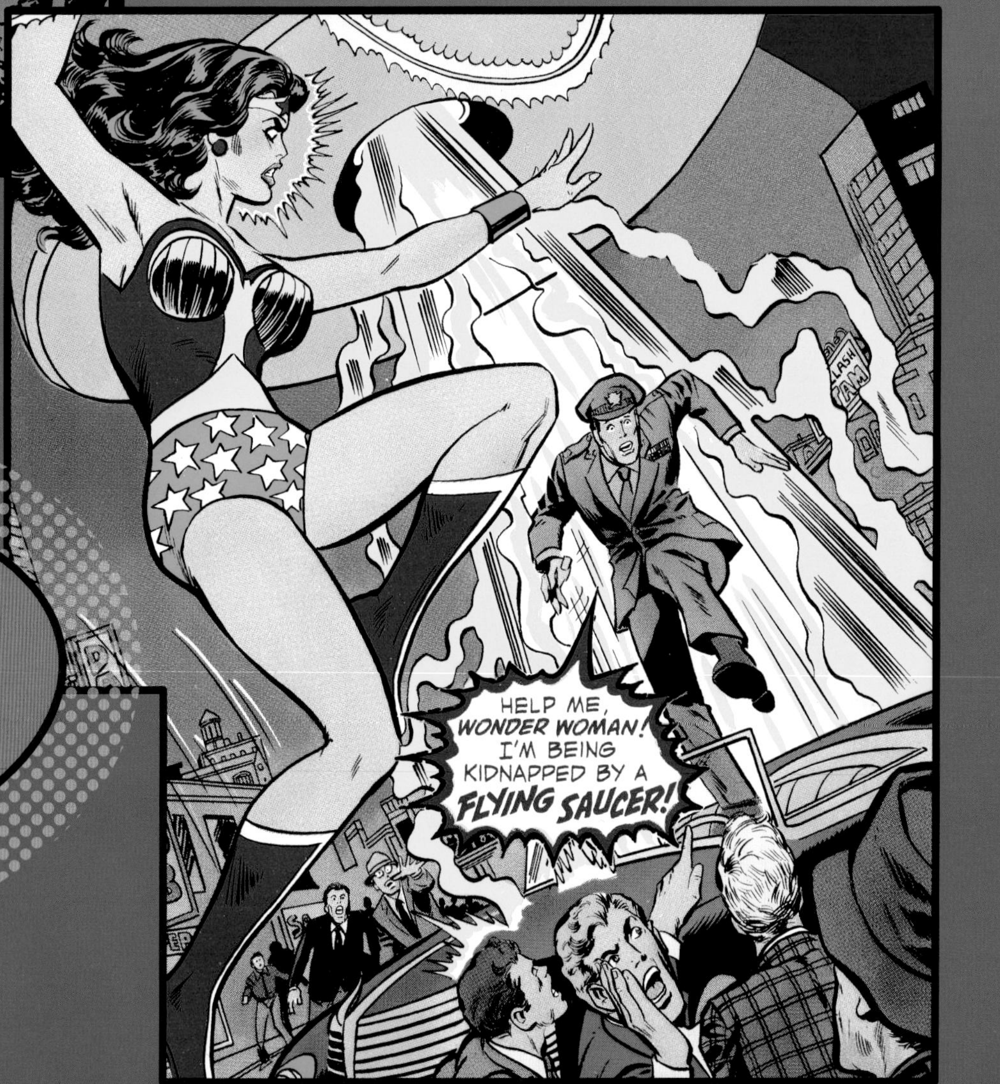
HELP ME, WONDER WOMAN! I'M BEING KIDNAPPED BY A FLYING SAUCER!

AMAZING ACCOMPLISHMENTS

Wonder Woman has outsmarted and overpowered anyone who has dared to break the law or harm others.

She even ran for president! Wouldn't *you* vote for her?

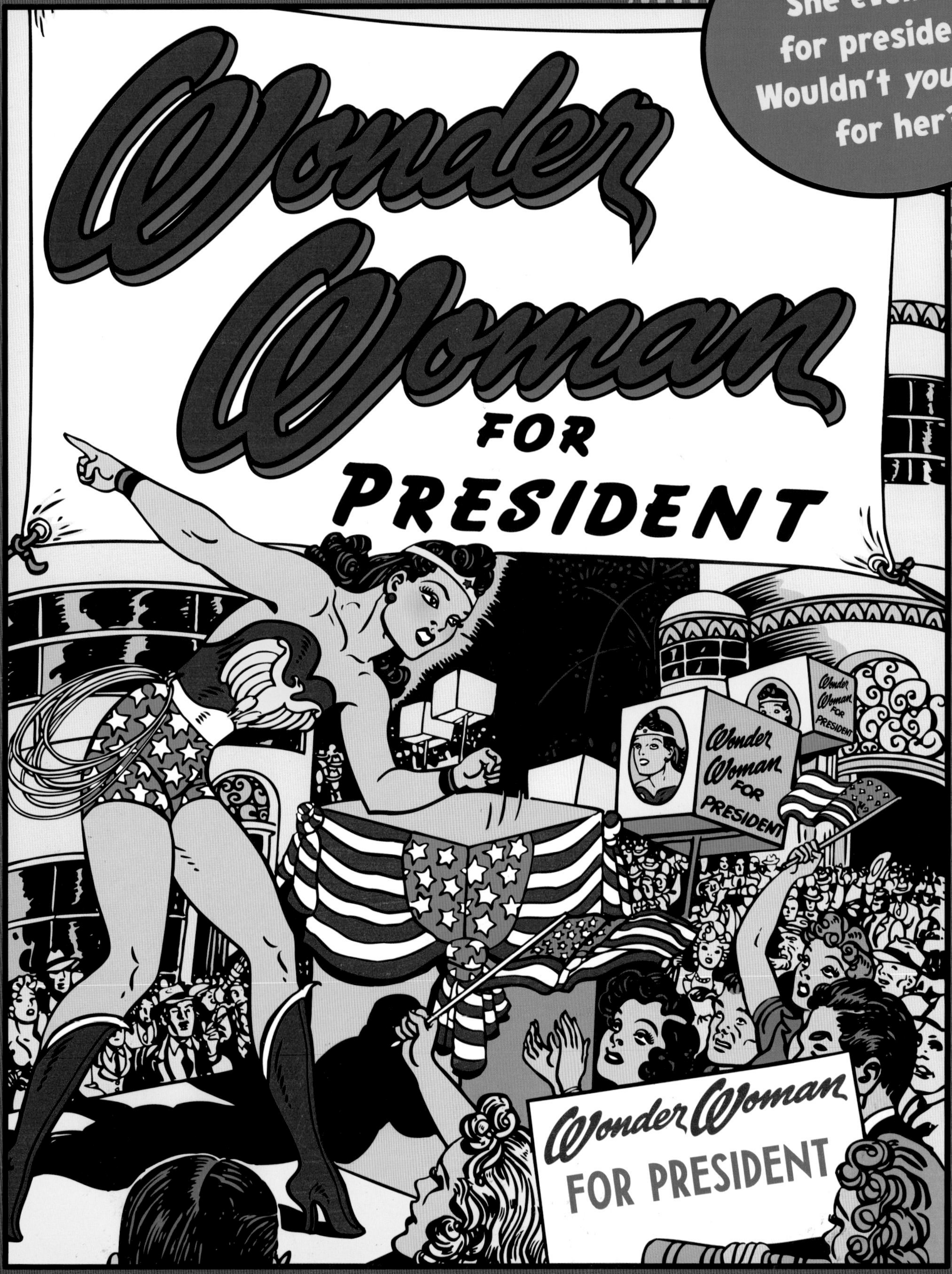

Wonder Woman
FOR
PRESIDENT
Wonder Woman
FOR
PRESIDENT
Wonder Woman
FOR
PRESIDENT
Wonder Woman
FOR PRESIDENT

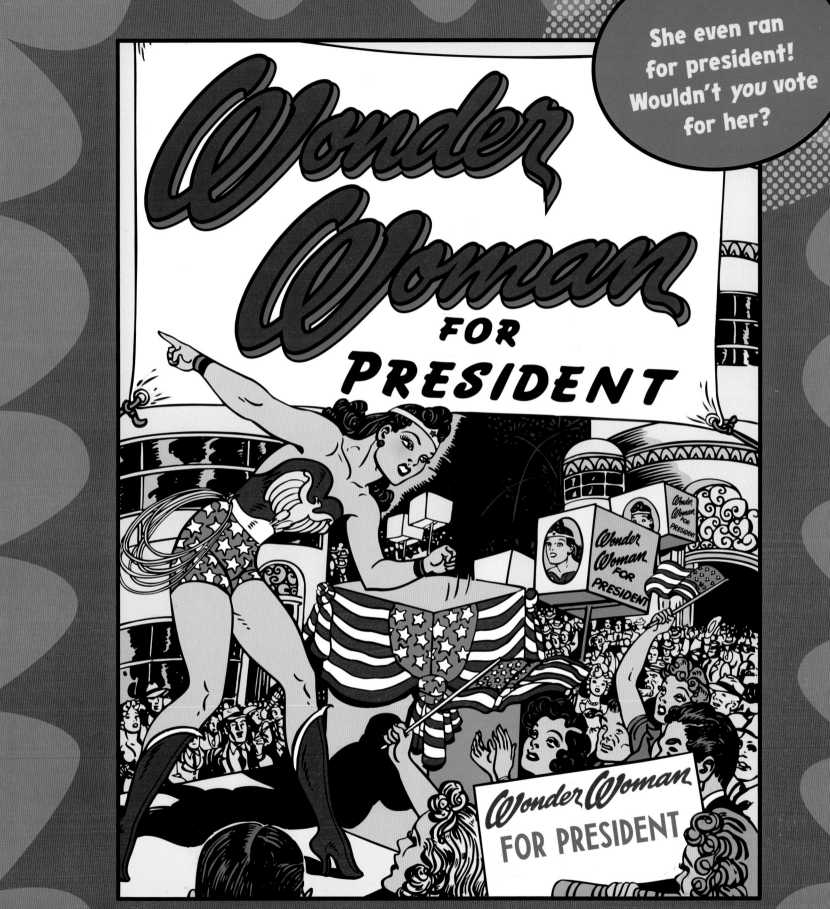

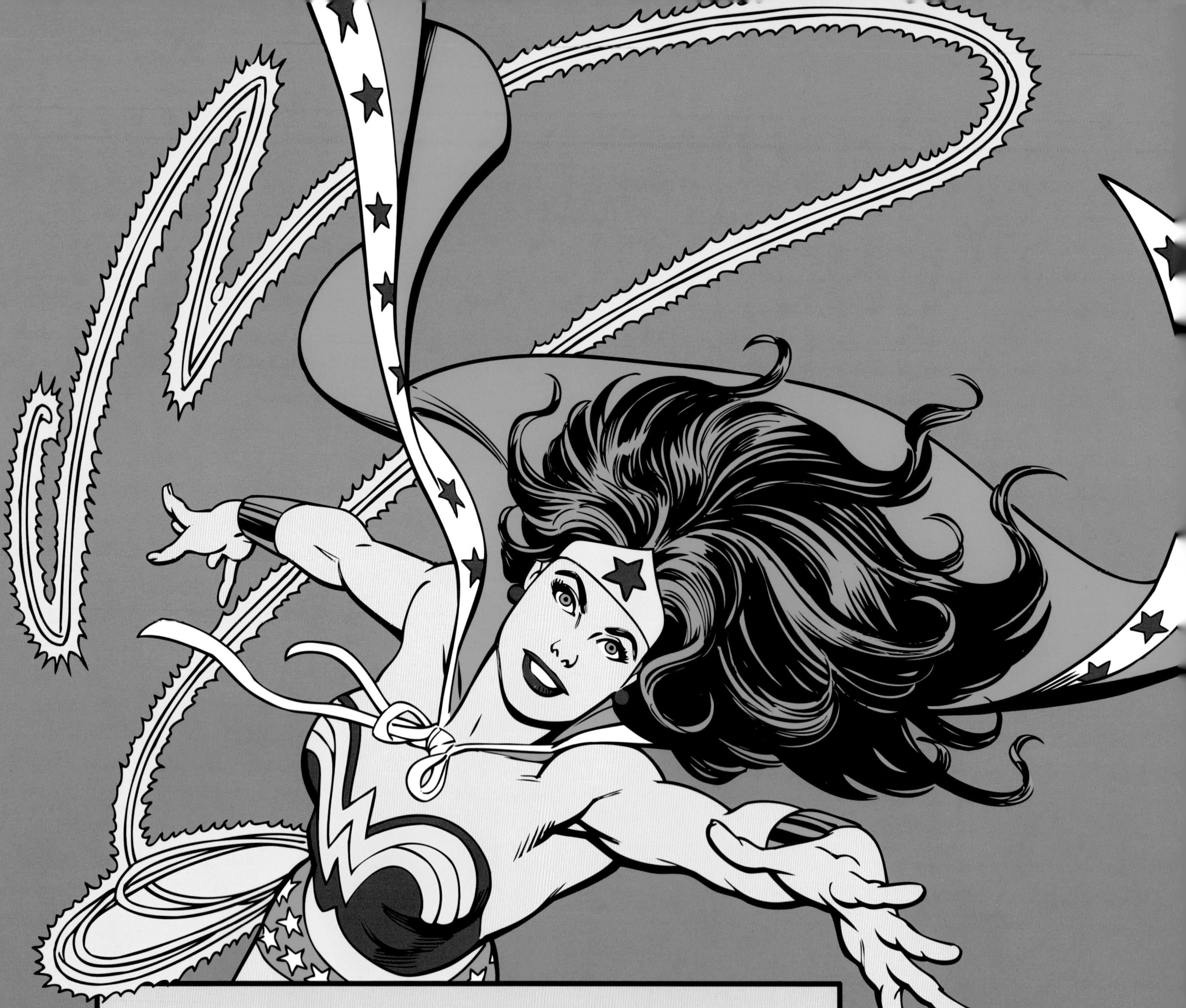

Every day, Wonder Woman finds ways to make the world a better place. She is always thinking: *Who can I help? Where am I needed? How can I make a difference?*

What are your special powers? How will you use them?